carol ann duffy

The Princess's Blankets

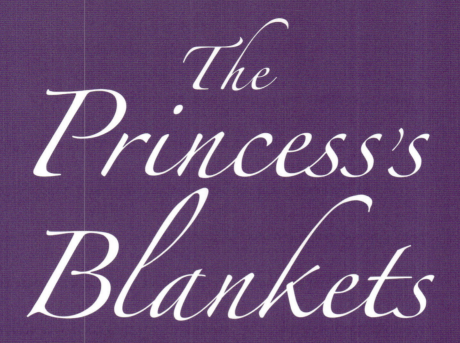

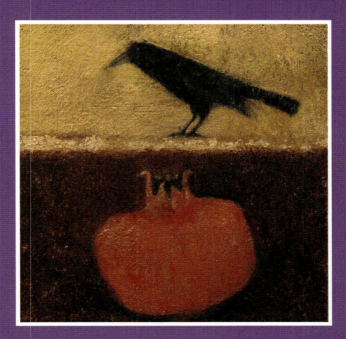

paintings by
catherine hyde

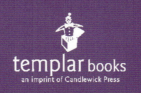

templar books
an imprint of Candlewick Press

t h e

❧ the bright sun   ❧ever

❧the princess staye

❧the ocean's blanket   ❧the forest

❧the earth's blanket   ❧th

❧the wonderful musi

❧the roaring, glittering sea   ❧t

❧under a blanke

paintings

the bright sun

A princess lived, once, who was always cold.

Even when the bright sun was at its hottest, she never felt warm. Her father,

the king, ordered huge, roaring fires to be lit in every room of the palace, but

although this made the royal servants so hot that the sweat dripped from the ends

of their noses and splashed onto the marble floors, the princess remained in her

bed. Her mother, the queen, instructed that the princess was always to be dressed

in the heaviest fleeces and the warmest woolens. And though every dressmaker in

the land stitched and sewed the warmest garments, and whole flocks of sheep

shivered fleeceless out in their fields, the princess stayed cold.

every dressmaker in the land

One day, the king announced that anyone who could think of a way to stop the princess from feeling so cold would be rewarded in any manner he or she chose, even unto half the kingdom. People came from far and wide carrying hot-water bottles plump with boiling water, or bearing bright copper warming pans crammed with glowing coals. They brought nightcaps, nightgowns, thermal underwear, bed socks, and sleeping gloves. Families emptied their drawers and chests of bed linens and blankets and made their way hopefully up to the palace. But it was all useless. The princess stayed shivering in her bed, dressed from head to toe in wool and fleeces—shawled, gloved, hatted, and scarfed, complaining of the cold.

the princess stayed shivering

It was nearing dusk one evening when a

stranger arrived at the palace demanding to

see the king. The man was dressed in black

clothes and did not bow when the king

entered. He had hard, gray eyes like polished

stones. He explained to the king that he knew

magic and could stop the princess's suffering.

If he was successful, as he was certain he

would be, he planned to carry the princess

back to his own land to be his wife.

When the queen heard that the stranger

was planning to take the princess away

should he earn his reward, she was unhappy

and remonstrated with the king. She was

sure her daughter would not care to be the

wife of a man with such stony eyes. But the

king said that the stranger should have his

chance, and it would be the price the

princess would have to pay to find warmth.

The stranger was escorted to the princess's bedchamber and stood before her. The princess was

sitting up in bed, wrapped in a fleece. The man told her why he was there and that soon he hoped to

win her for his wife. The princess felt afraid, for the stranger had cruel eyes, and even though she

longed to feel warm, she hoped that he would not be the person who would cure her.

"How cold do you feel?" asked the stranger.

I shall make it difficult for this arrogant man, thought the princess. So she answered, "As cold as

the ocean is."

The stranger gave a small smile and turned on his heel. He was gone for some time, and although the princess was freezing, she was glad to think she had gotten rid of the proud man. But no sooner

had she thought this than he appeared again in her room. He flung a huge blanket onto her bed.

The princess gasped as the blanket swamped her. It was woven in blues and greens and grays, and it

moved over her body in clumsy, urgent waves. It smelled salty and seaweedy as she tossed her head

on the pillow, and when she looked closer at the pattern on the blanket, she saw that many fish swam

in it and that dolphins leaped in its borders. There were whales in the blanket, and sad, sunken ships.

There were octopuses and jellyfish. The blanket lapped at her, and she felt sick.

"THE OCEAN'S BLANKET," he said.

overleaf: *the ocean's blanket*

"Warmer now?" demanded the stranger.

But the princess was even colder than before, and she trembled in her bed.

I will not go with you, she thought. So she replied, "No. I am as cold as the forest is."

The man nodded at her and left the room. The princess lay in her bed, hoping that she had seen

the last of him, but soon enough she heard his footsteps at her door. He came into the bedchamber

and tossed a huge blanket over her.

The blanket was coarse and spiky, and as the princess tried to push it off, it scratched at her arms

and hands, drawing blood. It was roughly woven in blacks and browns and dark greens. The blanket

smelled mossy and damp, and the princess saw that it was patterned with ancient trees and birds of

prey and embroidered with dark undergrowth and small, wild creatures.

"THE FOREST'S BLANKET," he said.

There was darkness in the blanket; there were frightening shadows. There were brambles and

snakes. The blanket clawed at her, and she felt faint.

"Warmer now?" asked the stranger.

But she was colder than ever, and her teeth were chattering.

You will not win me, thought the princess. Then she replied, "No. I am as cold as the mountain is."

The man looked angry, but he turned and strode from the room. He was gone for quite a while,

and the princess began to hope that he would not return. But the hope froze in her heart as she saw

the stranger enter her bedchamber yet again. He threw a great blanket over her bed. The blanket

was so heavy that the princess could hardly breathe as it pressed down on her. It was woven in many

different grays and shot through with sparkling silver. She pushed against it with her hands, but it was

as hard as stone and as jagged as rock, and her fine nails broke against it. She looked down and saw

the pattern of sheer cliffs and glaciers. There were ice-cold streams in the blanket, and dark ravines.

Frozen snow was heaped in its borders. The blanket bore down on her, and she felt dizzy.

"THE MOUNTAIN'S BLANKET," he said.

overleaf: the mountain's blanket

"Warmer now?" demanded the stranger.

But the princess was like ice and shivered on her bed.

I will not be yours, she thought. So she said, "No. I am as cold as the earth."

The stranger stared at her, then walked from the room. A long time passed, and the princess

prayed that he was gone for good. But even as the prayer formed on her pale lips, the man stood

before her once more. He lifted a huge blanket in his arms and spread it over her.

The princess moaned as the blanket came down over her, covering even her face. It smelled of dead

leaves and decay and felt moist and clammy. She pulled it from her face, feeling its soft, crumbly texture

in her hands. The blanket was woven in the darkest brown. It was patterned with worms and spiders,

and embroidered with corms and bulbs. There were tangled roots in the blanket; pale, hollow skulls;

and the crumbling bones of dead creatures. The blanket clung to her like a shroud, and she felt weak.

"THE EARTH'S BLANKET," he said.

overleaf: *the earth's blanket*

"Warmer now?" asked the man.

There was no reply.

"How cold?" demanded the stranger. "How cold now?"

But the princess was too cold to answer him, and the furious man had no choice but to leave the bedchamber and wait in the palace corridor until there was further news.

And now the people were sad and frightened because there was no ocean to fish in. The ocean was one of the princess's blankets, and all the empty fishing boats lay uselessly on the sands and mud flats, and folk went hungry for fish. Nor was there any longer a forest to pick fruit from or hunt in, or to chop and gather wood from to make fire.

The forest was one of the princess's blankets, and there were no trees left and no birds to sing in them. And the mountain was gone. The mountain was one of the princess's blankets, so there were no high peaks to collect rain from the clouds and no mountain streams bringing fresh water tumbling down to the towns and villages. There was no earth. The earth was one of the princess's blankets, so there were no vegetables growing in the soil, no corn or wheat swaying in the breeze, no colorful flowers or cool green grass. And if somebody died, their poor loved ones had nowhere to bury them. Word passed from ear to ear that all this had come about because the princess would not love the man with stony eyes.

One evening in late summer, a musician was walking quite near to the palace, playing on his flute. He was new to the country and wondered why the land was so bleak and arid, and why the people were so gloomy. He stopped for a while at an inn and came to hear about the cold princess. He heard about the terrible magic done by the stranger and how none of it had made the princess warm. The musician had a kind and good heart, and he made up his mind to go to the palace himself to see if he could help. He bowed before the sad king and kissed the hand of the tearful queen, and then he was led into the bedchamber, where the cold princess lay beneath her blankets of ocean and forest and mountain and earth.

As soon as he looked at her and saw how beautiful she was and how cold, the musician's heart flooded with love, and he was lost. He took out his flute and began to play the loveliest tune he knew, playing with his soul so that she would know how much he loved her. After a little while, the princess turned her head on the pillow and looked toward him. The musician played on until the princess sat up a little, listening intently to the wonderful music. She pulled her shawls tightly around her shoulders. When he had played the last note of his melody, the musician put down his flute and knelt by the side of the princess's bed. He took her cold hands from where they lay on the blanket and kissed each one with his warm lips, fingertip by fingertip. As he did so, the princess felt his warmth flood into her fingers, so that their skin burned with a surge of life and energy. She reached out and touched his hair with her tingling hands. As she did, the earth's blanket slipped from the bed. Then the musician kissed the princess's pale cheeks, and the princess flushed as she felt his warm breath on her face. She put her arms around the musician's neck to hide her blushes, and the mountain's blanket slid to the floor.

The musician heard the princess sigh in his ear and thought he would die with love, but he

took her face in his hands and kissed her eyelids. Two warm tears trickled down the princess's

face, and the forest's blanket slipped from the bed. The musician and the princess looked into

each other's eyes and they saw their souls there, and when the musician kissed her on the lips,

the princess's heart warmed her whole body with love. The ocean's blanket lay on the floor.

Outside, the roaring, glittering sea rushed in

foaming white waves for the shore, and the shouting,

pointing fishermen ran to their boats. The forest

shook the birds from its hair, tossing its leaves and

branches in the wind, shadowy and dark at the edge

of the town. Farther away, the huge mountain towered

against the skyline, its snowy peaks covered in cloud,

as though it were deep in thought. Later, as evening

began to fall, the fertile earth grew blurred and soft,

nurturing the growing harvest, nourishing its scented

flowers, nursing its dead.

The people went back to their ordinary lives,

grateful for the earth and the ocean, for the forest

and the mountain. The stranger was not heard of

again, although from time to time there were rumors

that he had drowned, or had fallen from a great height;

that he had been crushed by a tree, or been buried

alive. The king, with the queen beside him, kept his

word and told the musician to name his reward. The

musician only asked to stay always by the princess's

side, and the princess agreed.

the stranger was not heard of again

Sometimes,

on summer nights, they slept outside, hearing

the mountain stream and the sea and the wind

in the trees, under a blanket of stars.

under a blanket of stars

For Vivien
C.A.D.

For my parents,
John and Marina,
with my love
C.H.

Text copyright © 2008 by Carol Ann Duffy
Illustrations copyright © 2008 by Catherine Hyde

First U.S. edition 2009

Library of Congress Cataloging-in-Publication Data is available.
Library of Congress Catalog Card Number 2008938414
ISBN 978-0-7636-4547-2

2 4 6 8 10 9 7 5 3 1

Printed in China

This book was typeset in GillSans. • The illustrations were done in acrylic on canvas with copper, gold, and silver leaf.

Edited by Stella Gurney • Designed by Janie Louise Hunt

A TEMPLAR BOOK

an imprint of
Candlewick Press
99 Dover Street
Somerville, Massachusetts 02144
www.candlewick.com

In memory of
the Solomon Browne.
For L. B. with love
J.L.H.